# DRUMMER HOFF

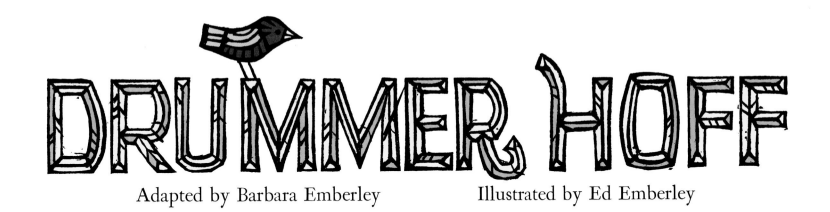

# DRUMMER HOFF

Adapted by Barbara Emberley    Illustrated by Ed Emberley

Aladdin Paperbacks

Aladdin Paperbacks
An imprint of Simon & Schuster Children's Publishing Division
1230 Avenue of the Americas
New York, NY 10020

Manufactured in China

40

Library of Congress Cataloging-in-Publication Data

Emberley, Barbara.
Drummer Hoff.
Summary: A cumulative folk song in which seven
soldiers build a magnificent cannon, but Drummer
Hoff fires it off.
[1. Folk songs]   I. Emberley, Ed. ill.   II. Title.
PZ8.3.E515Dr 1987      784.4'05   87-35755
ISBN 0-671-66248-1   ISBN 0-671-66249-X (pbk.)

Drummer Hoff fired it off.

Private Parriage
brought the carriage,

but Drummer Hoff fired it off.

Corporal Farrell
brought the barrel.

Corporal Farrell
brought the barrel,
Private Parriage
brought the carriage,
but Drummer Hoff
fired it off.

Sergeant Chowder
brought the powder.

Sergeant Chowder
brought the powder,
Corporal Farrell
brought the barrel,
Private Parriage
brought the carriage,
but Drummer Hoff
fired it off.

Captain Bammer
brought the rammer.

Captain Bammer
brought the rammer,
Sergeant Chowder
brought the powder,
Corporal Farrell
brought the barrel,
Private Parriage
brought the carriage,
but Drummer Hoff fired it off.

Major Scott
brought the shot.

Major Scott brought the shot,
Captain Bammer
brought the rammer,
Sergeant Chowder
brought the powder,
Corporal Farrell
brought the barrel,
Private Parriage
brought the carriage,
but Drummer Hoff fired it off.

General Border
gave the order.

General Border
gave the order,
Major Scott
brought the shot,
Captain Bammer
brought the rammer,
Sergeant Chowder
brought the powder,
Corporal Farrell
brought the barrel,
Private Parriage
brought the carriage,
but Drummer Hoff fired it off.